Classic Nonsense Verse

D1136836

PENGUIN BOOKS

PENGUIN BOOKS

Published by the Penguin Group
Penguin Books Ltd, 27 Wrights Lane, London w8 5tz, England
Penguin Books USA Inc., 375 Hudson Street, New York, New York 10014, USA
Penguin Books Australia Ltd, Ringwood, Victoria, Australia
Penguin Books Canada Ltd, 10 Alcorn Avenue, Toronto, Ontario, Canada m4v 3b2
Penguin Books (NZ) Ltd, 182–190 Wairau Road, Auckland 10, New Zealand

Penguin Books Ltd, Registered Offices: Harmondsworth, Middlesex, England

First published 1996
1 3 5 7 9 10 8 6 4 2

Set in 11/14 Monophoto Bembo
Typeset by Datix International Limited, Bungay, Suffolk
Printed in England by Clays Ltd, St Ives plc

Contents

I Saw a Peacock

I saw a peacock with a fiery tail
I saw a blazing comet pour down hail
I saw a cloud all wrapt with ivy round
I saw a lofty oak creep on the ground
I saw a beetle swallow up a whale
I saw a foaming sea brimful of ale
I saw a pewter cup sixteen feet deep
I saw a well full of men's tears that weep
I saw wet eyes in flames of living fire
I saw a house as high as the moon and higher
I saw the glorious sun at deep midnight
I saw the man who saw this wondrous sight.

ANONYMOUS

1

One Fine Day in the Middle of the Night

One fine day in the middle of the night,
Two dead men got up to fight,
Back to back they faced each other,
Drew their swords and shot each other.
A paralysed donkey passing by
Kicked a blind man in the eye,
Knocked him through a nine-inch wall
Into a dry ditch and drowned them all.

ANONYMOUS

I Went to the Pictures Tomorrow

I went to the pictures tomorrow
I took a front seat at the back,
I fell from the pit to the gallery
And broke a front bone in my back.
A lady she gave me some chocolate,
I ate it and gave it her back.
I phoned for a taxi and walked it,
And that's why I never came back.

PLAYGROUND RHYME

When I Went Out for a Walk One Day

When I went out for a walk one day,
   My head fell off and rolled away,
And when I saw that it was gone –
   I picked it up and put it on.

When I went into the street
   Someone shouted, 'Look at your feet!'
I looked at them and sadly said,
   'I've left them both asleep in bed!'

ANONYMOUS

Jabberwocky

'Twas brillig, and the slithy toves
    Did gyre and gimble in the wabe;
All mimsy were the borogoves,
    And the mome raths outgrabe.

'Beware the Jabberwock, my son!
    The jaws that bite, the claws that catch!
Beware the Jubjub bird, and shun
    The frumious Bandersnatch!'

He took his vorpal sword in hand:
    Long time the manxome foe he sought –
So rested he by the Tumtum tree,
    And stood awhile in thought.

And as in uffish thought he stood,
    The Jabberwock, with eyes of flame,
Came whiffling through the tulgey wood,
    And burbled as it came!

One, two! One, two! And through and through
    The vorpal blade went snicker-snack!
He left it dead, and with its head
    He went galumphing back.

'And hast thou slain the Jabberwock?
    Come to my arms, my beamish boy!
O frabjous day! Callooh! Callay!'
    He chortled in his joy.

'Twas brillig, and the slithy toves
    Did gyre and gimble in the wabe;
All mimsy were the borogoves,
    And the mome raths outgrabe.

LEWIS CARROLL

To Marie

When the breeze from the bluebottle's blustering
   blim
      Twirls the toads in a tooroomaloo,
And the whiskery whine of the wheedlesome whim
      Drowns the roll of the rattatattoo,
Then I dream in the shade of the shally-go-shee,
      And the voice of the bally-molay
Brings the smell of the pale poppy-cod's blummered
   blee
      From the willy-wad over the way.

Ah, the shuddering shoe and the blinketty-blanks
      When the punglung falls from the bough
In the blast of a hurricane's hicketty-hanks
      O'er the hills of the hocketty-how!
Give the rigamarole to the clangery-whang,
      If they care for such fiddlededee;
But the thingumbob kiss of the whangery-bang
      Keeps the higgledy-piggle for me.

from MELODIES

There was once a young man of Oporta
Who daily got shorter and shorter,
   The reason he said
   Was the hod on his head,
Which was filled with the *heaviest* mortar.

His sister named Lucy O'Finner,
Grew constantly thinnner and thinner,
      The reason was plain,
      She slept out in the rain,
And was never allowed any dinner.

LEWIS CARROLL

Belagcholly Days

Chilly Dovebber with his boadigg blast
   Dow cubs add strips the bedow add the lawd,
Eved October's suddy days are past —
   Add Subber's gawd!

I kdow dot what it is to which I cligg
   That stirs to sogg add sorrow, yet I trust
That still I sigg, but as the liddets sigg —
   Because I bust.

Add now, farewell to roses add to birds,
   To larded fields and tigkligg streablets eke;
Farewell to all articulated words
   I fain would speak.

Farewell, by cherished strolliggs od the sward,
   Greed glades and forest shades, farewell to you;
With sorrowing heart I, wretched add forlord,
   Bid you – achew!!!

ANONYMOUS

There Was an Old Person of Slough

There was an Old Person of Slough,
who danced at the end of a Bough;
But they said, 'If you sneeze,
you might damage the trees,
You imprudent Old Person of Slough.'

EDWARD LEAR

Jerry Hall

Jerry Hall
Is so small,
A rat could eat him
Hat and all.

ANONYMOUS

There Was a Mad Man

There was a Mad Man,
And he had a Mad Wife,
And they lived in a Mad town,
They had three Children
All at a Birth,
And they were Mad
Every One.

The Father was Mad,
The Mother was Mad,
The Children all Mad besides,
And they all got
Upon a Mad Horse,
And Madly they did ride.

They rode by night and they rode by day,
Yet never a one of them fell,
They rode so madly all the way,
Till they came to the gates of hell.

Old Nick was glad to see them so mad,
And gladly let them in:
But he soon grew sorry to see him so merry,
And let them out again.

ANONYMOUS

Brother and Sister

'Sister, sister, go to bed,
Go and rest your weary head,'
Thus the prudent brother said.

'Do you want a battered hide
Or scratches to your face applied?'
Thus the sister calm replied.

'Sister! do not rouse my wrath,
I'd make you into mutton broth
As easily as kill a moth.'

The sister raised her beaming eye,
And looked on him indignantly,
And sternly answered 'Only try!'

Off to the cook he quickly ran,
'Dear cook, pray lend a frying pan
To me, as quickly as you can.'

'And wherefore should I give it you?'
'The reason, cook, is plain to view,
I wish to make an Irish stew.'

'What meat is in that stew to go?'
'My sister'll be the contents.' 'Oh!'
'Will you lend the pan, cook?' 'NO!'

MORAL
'Never stew your sister.'

LEWIS CARROLL

A Sunnit to the Big Ox

(*Composed while standing within two feet of him, and a tuchin' of him now and then.*)

All hale! thou mighty annimil all hale!
You are 4 thousand pounds, and am purty wel
Perporshund, thou tremendjus boveen nuggit!
I wonder how big yu was when yu
Was little, and if yure mother would no yu now
That yu've grone so long, and thick and fat;
Or if yure father would rekognise his ofspring
And his kaff, thou elephanteen quadrupid!
I wonder if it hurts yu much to be so big,
And if yu grode it in a month or so.
I spose wen yu was young tha didn't gin
Yu skim milk but all the creme yu could stuff
Into yore little stummick, jest to see
How big yu'd gro; and afterward tha no doubt
Fed yu on oats and hay and sich like,
With perhaps an occasional punkin or squosh!
In all probability yu don't know yure anny

Bigger than a small kaff; for if yu did
Yude break down fences and switch yure tail,
And rush around and hook and beller,
And run over fowkes, thou orful beast.
O, what a lot of mince pies yude maik,
And sassengers, and your tail,
Whitch can't weigh fur from forty pounds,
Wud maik nigh unto a barrel of ox-tail soup,
And cudn't a heep of staiks be cut off you,
Whitch, with salt and pepper and termater
Ketchup, wouldn't be bad to taik.
Thou grate and glorious inseckt!
But I must close, O most prodijus reptile!
And for mi admiration of yu, when yu di,
I'le rite a node unto yure peddy and remanes,
Pernouncin yu the largest of yure race;
And as I don't expec to have half a dollar
Again to spair for to pay to look at yu, and as
I ain't a dead head, I will sa, farewell.

ANONYMOUS

18

Some Verses to Snaix

Prodiggus reptile! long and skaly kuss!
You are the dadrattedest biggest thing I ever
Seed that cud ty itself into a double bo-
Not, and cum all strate again in a
Minnit or so, without winkin or seemin
To experience any particular pane
In the diafram.

Stoopenjus inseck! marvelous annimile!
You are no doubt seven thousand yeres
Old, and hav a considerable of a
Family sneekin round thru the tall
Gras in Africa, a eetin up little greezy
Piggers, and wishin they was biggir.

I wonder how big yu was when yu
Was a inphant about 2 fete long. I
Expec yu was a purty good size, and
Lived on phrogs, and lizzerds, and polly-
Wogs and sutch things.

You are havin' a nice time now, ennyhow –
Don't have nothing to do but lay oph.
And ete kats and rabbits, and stic
Out yure tung and twist yur tale.
I wunder if yu ever swollered a man
Without takin oph his butes. If there was
Brass buttins on his kote, I spose

Yu had ter swaller a lot of buttin-
Wholes, and a shu-hamer to nock
The soals oph of the boots and drive in
The tax, so that they would n't kut yure
Inside. I wunder if vittles taste
Good all the way down. I expec so –
At leest, fur 6 or 7 fete.

You are so mighty long, I shud thynk
If your tale was kold, yure hed
Woodent no it till the next day,
But it's hard tu tell: snaix is snaix.

ANONYMOUS

The Owl and the Pussy-cat

[I]

The Owl and the Pussy-cat went to sea
    In a beautiful pea-green boat,
They took some honey, and plenty of money,
    Wrapped up in a five-pound note.
The Owl looked up to the stars above,
    And sang to a small guitar,
'O lovely Pussy! O Pussy, my love,
        What a beautiful Pussy you are,
            You are,
            You are!
    What a beautiful Pussy you are!'

[II]

Pussy said to the Owl, 'You elegant fowl!
    How charmingly sweet you sing!
O let us be married! too long we have tarried:
    But what shall we do for a ring?'
They sailed away, for a year and a day,

To the land where the Bong-tree grows
And there in a wood a Piggy-wig stood
With a ring at the end of his nose,
His nose,
His nose,
With a ring at the end of his nose.

[III]

'Dear Pig, are you willing to sell for one shilling
Your ring?' Said the Piggy, 'I will.'
So they took it away, and were married next day
By the Turkey who lives on the hill.
They dined on mince, and slices of quince,
Which they ate with a runcible spoon;
And hand in hand, on the edge of the sand,
They danced by the light of the moon,
The moon,
The moon,
They danced by the light of the moon.

EDWARD LEAR

A Chronicle

Once – but no matter when –
   There lived – no matter where –
A man, whose name – but then
   I need not that declare.

He – well, he had been born,
   And so he was alive;
His age – I details scorn –
   Was somethingty and five.

He lived – how many years
   I truly can't decide;
But this one fact appears
   He lived – until he died.

'He died,' I have averred,
   But cannot prove 't was so,
But that he was interred,
   At any rate, I know.

I fancy he'd a son,
   I hear he had a wife:
Perhaps he'd more than one,
   I know not, on my life!

But whether he was rich,
   Or whether he was poor,
Or neither – both – or which,
   I cannot say, I'm sure.

I can't recall his name,
   Or what he used to do:
But then – well, such is fame!
   'T will so serve me and you.

And that is why I thus,
   About this unknown man
Would fain create a fuss,
   To rescue, if I can.

From dark oblivion's blow,
   Some record of his lot:
But, ah! I do not know
   Who – where – when – why – or what.

MORAL

In this brief pedigree
   A moral we should find –
But what it ought to be
   Has quite escaped my mind!

ANONYMOUS

The Mad Gardener's Song

He thought he saw an Elephant,
   That practised on a fife:
He looked again, and found it was
   A letter from his wife.
'At length I realise,' he said,
   'The bitterness of Life!'

He thought he saw a Buffalo
   Upon the chimney-piece:
He looked again, and found it was
   His Sister's Husband's Niece.
'Unless you leave this house,' he said,
   'I'll send for the Police!'

He thought he saw a Rattlesnake
   That questioned him in Greek:
He looked again, and found it was
   The Middle of Next Week.
'The only thing I regret,' he said,

'Is that it cannot speak!'

He thought he saw a Banker's Clerk
    Descending from the bus:
He looked again, and found it was
    A Hippopotamus:
'If this should stay to dine,' he said,
    'There won't be much for us!'

He thought he saw a Kangaroo
    That worked a coffee-mill:
He looked again, and found it was
    A Vegetable-Pill.
'Were I to swallow this,' he said,
    'I should be very ill!'

He thought he saw a Coach-and-Four
    That stood beside his bed:
He looked again, and found it was
    A Bear without a Head.
'Poor thing,' he said, 'poor silly thing!
    It's waiting to be fed!'

He thought he saw an Albatross
    That fluttered round the lamp:
He looked again, and found it was
    A Penny-Postage-Stamp.
'You'd best be getting home,' he said:
    'The nights are very damp!'

He thought he saw a Garden-Door
    That opened with a key:
He looked again, and found it was
    A Double Rule of Three:
'And all its mystery,' he said,
    'Is clear as day to me!'

He thought he saw an Argument
    That proved he was the Pope:
He looked again, and found it was
    A Bar of Mottled Soap.
'A fact so dread,' he faintly said,
    'Extinguishes all hope!'

LEWIS CARROLL

As I Went Over the Water

As I went over the water,
    The water went over me.
I saw two little blackbirds
    Sitting on a tree:
The one called me a rascal,
    The other called me a thief;
I took up my little black stick,
    And knocked out all their teeth.

ANONYMOUS

Goosey, Goosey, Gander

Goosey, goosey, gander,
　Where shall I wander?
Upstairs, downstairs,
　And in my lady's chamber.
There I met an old man
　Who would not say his prayers;
I took him by the left leg
　And threw him down the stairs.

ANONYMOUS

Little Willie's Dead

Little Willie's dead,
Jam him in the coffin,
For you don't get the chance
Of a funeral of 'en.

ANONYMOUS

The Walrus and the Carpenter

The sun was shining on the sea
    Shining with all his might:
He did his very best to make
    The billows smooth and bright –
And this was odd, because it was
    The middle of the night.

The moon was shining sulkily,
    Because she thought the sun
Had got no business to be there
    After the day was done –
'It's very rude of him,' she said,
    'To come and spoil the fun!'

The sea was wet as wet could be,
    The sands were dry as dry.
You could not see a cloud, because
    No cloud was in the sky:
No birds were flying overhead –

There were no birds to fly.

The Walrus and the Carpenter
    Were walking close at hand;
They wept like anything to see
    Such quantities of sand:
'If this were only cleared away,'
    They said, 'it *would* be grand!'

'If seven maids with seven mops
    Swept it for half a year,
Do you suppose,' the Walrus said,
    'That they could get it clear?'
'I doubt it,' said the Carpenter,
    And shed a bitter tear.

'O Oysters, come and walk with us!'
    The Walrus did beseech.
'A pleasant walk, a pleasant talk,
    Along the briny beach:
We cannot do with more than four,
    To give a hand to each.'

The eldest Oyster looked at him,
    But never a word he said:
The eldest Oyster winked his eye,
    And shook his heavy head –
Meaning to say he did not choose
    To leave the oyster-bed.

But four young Oysters hurried up,
    All eager for the treat:
Their coats were brushed, their faces washed,
    Their shoes were clean and neat –
And this was odd, because, you know,
    They hadn't any feet.

Four other Oysters followed them,
    And yet another four;
And thick and fast they came at last,
    And more, and more, and more –
All hopping through the frothy waves,
    And scrambling to the shore.

The Walrus and the Carpenter
    Walked on a mile or so.
And then they rested on a rock
    Conveniently low:
And all the little Oysters stood
    And waited in a row.

'The time has come,' the Walrus said,
    'To talk of many things:
Of shoes – and ships – and sealing-wax –
    Of cabbages – and kings –
And why the sea is boiling hot –
    And whether pigs have wings.'

'But wait a bit,' the Oysters cried,
    'Before we have our chat;
For some of us are out of breath,
    And all of us are fat!'
'No hurry!' said the Carpenter.
    They thanked him much for that.

'A loaf of bread,' the Walrus said,
   'Is what we chiefly need:
Pepper and vinegar besides
   Are very good indeed –
Now if you're ready, Oysters dear,
   We can begin to feed.'

'But not on us!' the Oysters cried,
   Turning a little blue.
'After such kindness, that would be
   A dismal thing to do!'
'The night is fine,' the Walrus said.
   'Do you admire the view?'

'It was so kind of you to come!
   And you are very nice!'
The Carpenter said nothing but
   'Cut us another slice:
I wish you were not quite so deaf –
   I've had to ask you twice!'

'It seems a shame,' the Walrus said,
    'To play them such a trick,
After we've brought them out so far,
    And made them trot so quick!'
The Carpenter said nothing but
    'The butter's spread too thick!'

'I weep for you,' the Walrus said:
    'I deeply sympathize.'
With sobs and tears he sorted out
    Those of the largest size,
Holding his pocket-handkerchief
    Before his streaming eyes.

'O Oysters,' said the Carpenter,
    'You've had a pleasant run!
Shall we be trotting home again?'
    But answer came there none –
And this was scarcely odd, because
    They'd eaten every one.

LEWIS CARROLL

Said the Monkey to the Donkey

Said the monkey to the donkey,
'What'll you have to drink?'
Said the donkey to the monkey,
'I'd like a swig of ink.'

ANONYMOUS

A Cat Came Dancing Out of a Barn

A cat came dancing out of a barn
With a pair of bag-pipes under her arm;
She could sing nothing but, Fiddle cum fee,
The mouse has married the bumble-bee.
Pipe, cat; dance, mouse;
We'll have a wedding at our good house.

NURSERY RHYME

The Comic Adventures of
Old Mother Hubbard and Her Dog

Old Mother Hubbard
Went to the cupboard,
To fetch her poor dog a bone;
But when she came there
The cupboard was bare
And so the poor dog had none.

She went to the baker's
To buy him some bread;
But when she came back
The poor dog was dead.

She went to the undertaker's
To buy him a coffin;
But when she came back
The poor dog was laughing.

She took a clean dish
  To get him some tripe:
But when she came back
  He was smoking a pipe.

She went to the alehouse
  To get him some beer;
But when she came back
  The dog sat in a chair.

She went to the tavern
  For white wine and red;
But when she came back
  The dog stood on his head.

She went to the fruiterer's
  To buy him some fruit;
But when she came back
  He was playing the flute.

She went to the tailor's
  To buy him a coat;

But when she came back
  He was riding a goat.

She went to the hatter's
  To buy him a hat;
But when she came back
  He was feeding the cat.

She went to the barber's
  To buy him a wig;
But when she came back
  He was dancing a jig.

She went to the cobbler's
  To buy him some shoes:
But when she came back
  He was reading the news.

She went to the seamstress
  To buy him some linen;
But when she came back
  The dog was a-spinning.

She went to the hosier's
    To buy him some hose;
But when she came back
    He was dressed in his clothes.

The dame made a curtsey,
    The dog made a bow;
The dame said, Your servant,
    The dog said, Bow-wow.

ANONYMOUS

44

The Jumblies

They went to sea in a Sieve, they did,
   In a Sieve they went to sea:
In spite of all their friends could say,
On a winter's morn, on a stormy day,
   In a Sieve they went to sea!
And when the Sieve turned round and round,
And every one cried, 'You'll all be drowned!'
They called aloud, 'Our Sieve ain't big,
But we don't care a button! we don't care a fig!
   In a Sieve we'll go to sea!'
     Far and few, far and few,
       Are the lands where the Jumblies live;
       Their heads are green, and their hands are blue,
        And they went to sea in a Sieve.

[II]

They sailed in a Sieve, they did,
   In a Sieve they sailed so fast,

45

With only a beautiful pea-green veil
Tied with a riband by way of a sail,
   To a small tobacco-pipe mast;
And every one said, who saw them go,
'O won't they be soon upset, you know!
For the sky is dark, and the voyage is long,
And happen what may, it's extremely wrong
    In a Sieve to sail so fast!'
      Far and few, far and few,
        Are the lands where the Jumblies live;
        Their heads are green, and their hands are blue,
          And they went to sea in a Sieve.

[III]

The water it soon came in, it did,
   The water it soon came in;
So to keep them dry, they wrapped their feet
In a pinky paper all folded neat,
   And they fastened it down with a pin.
And they passed the night in a crockery-jar,
And each of them said, 'How wise we are!
Though the sky be dark, and the voyage be long,

Yet we never can think we were rash or wrong,
　　While round in our Sieve we spin!'
　　　Far and few, far and few,
　　　　Are the lands where the Jumblies live;
　　　　Their heads are green, and their hands are blue,
　　　　　And they went to sea in a Sieve.

[IV]

And all night long they sailed away;
　　And when the sun went down,
They whistled and warbled a moony song
To the echoing sound of a coppery gong,
　　In the shade of the mountains brown.
'O Timballo! How happy we are,
When we live in a sieve and a crockery-jar,
And all night long in the moonlight pale,
We sail away with a pea-green sail,
　　In the shade of the mountains brown!'
　　　Far and few, far and few,
　　　　Are the lands where the Jumblies live;
　　　　Their heads are green, and their hands are blue,
　　　　　And they went to sea in a Sieve.　　47

They sailed to the Western Sea, they did,
 To a land all covered with trees,
And they bought an Owl, and a useful Cart,
And a pound of Rice, and a Cranberry Tart,
 And a hive of silvery Bees.
And they bought a Pig, and some green Jack-daws,
And a lovely Monkey with lollipop paws,
And forty bottles of Ring-Bo-Ree,
 And no end of Stilton Cheese.
   Far and few, far and few,
    Are the lands where the Jumblies live;
    Their heads are green, and their hands are blue,
     And they went to sea in a Sieve.

[VI]

And in twenty years they all came back,
 In twenty years or more,
And every one said, 'How tall they've grown!
For they've been to the Lakes, and the Torrible
 Zone,
And the hills of the Chankly Bore';

And they drank their health, and gave them a feast
Of dumplings made of beautiful yeast;
And every one said, 'If we only live,
We too will go to sea in a Sieve, –
    To the hills of the Chankly Bore!'
        Far and few, far and few,
            Are the lands where the Jumblies live;
            Their heads are green, and their hands are blue,
                And they went to sea in a Sieve.

EDWARD LEAR

The Monkey's Wedding

The monkey married the Baboon's sister,
Smacked his lips and then he kissed her,
He kissed so hard he raised a blister.
      She set up a yell.
The bridesmaid stuck on some court plaster,
It stuck so fast it couldn't stick faster,
Surely 'twas a sad disaster,
      But it soon got well.

What do you think the bride was dressed in?
White gauze veil and a green glass breast-pin,
Red kid shoes – she was quite interesting,
      She was quite a belle.
The bridegroom swell'd with a blue shirt collar,
Black silk stock that cost a dollar,
Large false whiskers the fashion to follow;
      He cut a monstrous swell.

What do you think they had for supper?

Black-eyed peas and bread and butter,
Ducks in the duck-house all in a flutter
      Pickled oysters too.
Chestnuts raw and boil'd and roasted,
Apples sliced and onions toasted,
Music in the corner posted,
        Waiting for the cue.

What do you think was the tune they danced to?
'The drunken Sailor' – sometimes 'Jim Crow,'
Tails in the way – and some got pinched, too,
        'Cause they were too long.
What do you think they had for a fiddle?
An old Banjo with a hole in the middle,
A Tambourine made out of a riddle,
        And that's the end of my song.

ANONYMOUS

Simple Simon

Simple Simon went a-fishing
For to catch a whale;
All the water he had got
Was in his mother's pail.

Simple Simon went a-skating
On a pond in June.
'Dear me,' he cried, 'this water's wet,
I fear I've come too soon!'

Simple Simon made a snowball,
And brought it home to roast;
He laid it down before the fire,
And soon the ball was lost.

Simple Simon bought a gun,
'To shoot a bird,' he said.

He held the gun the wrong way round,
And shot himself instead.

ANONYMOUS

Calico Pie

Calico Pie,
  The little Birds fly
Down to the calico tree,
Their wings were blue,
And they sang 'Tilly-loo!'
Till away they flew, –
    And they never came back to me!
      They never came back!
      They never came back!
    They never came back to me!

      Calico Jam,
        The little Fish swam
    Over the syllabub sea,
      He took off his hat,
      To the Sole and the Sprat,
      And the Willeby-wat, –
    But he never came back to me!
He never came back!

He never came back!
He never came back to me!

Calico Ban,
The little Mice ran,
To be ready in time for tea,
Flippity flup,
They drank it all up,
And danced in the cup, –
But they never came back to me!
They never came back!
They never came back!
They never came back to me!

Calico Drum,
The Grasshoppers come,
The Butterfly, Beetle, and Bee,
Over the ground,
Around and round,
With a hop and a bound, –
But they never came back!
They never came back!

They never came back!
They never came back to me!

EDWARD LEAR

PENGUIN CHILDREN'S 60s

Some Puffin poetry books

GARGLING WITH JELLY *Brian Patten*
HE SAID, SHE SAID, THEY SAID *Anne Harvey* (Ed.)
HEARD IT IN THE PLAYGROUND *Allan Ahlberg*
I LIKE THIS POEM *Kaye Webb* (Ed.)
THE NEW PUFFIN BOOK OF FUNNY VERSE
Kit Wright (Ed.)
PLEASE MRS BUTLER *Allan Ahlberg*
RHYME STEW *Roald Dahl*
TWO'S COMPANY *Jackie Kay*
WOULDN'T YOU LIKE TO KNOW *Michael Rosen*
AN IMAGINARY MENAGERIE *Roger McGough*
SILLY VERSE FOR KIDS *Spike Milligan*
LAUGHTER IS AN EGG *John Agard*
WHEN I DANCE *James Berry*
EARLY IN THE MORNING *Charles Causley*
THIRD TIME LUCKY *Mick Gowar*
THE HOUSE THAT CAUGHT COLD *Richard Edwards*